THE PRINCESS AND THE PEA

THE PRINCESS AND THE PEA

This Book Belongs To:

_____

For information regarding permission write:
Books to Bed, Inc.
224 West 35th street, Room 700, New York, NY 10001

Library of Congress Cataloging-in-Publication Data on file
ISBN #978-1-4951-0590-6

First Edition

Importer: Books to Bed, Inc
Printed in China

Recommended for age3+

Visit us at www.Bookstobed.com

The Princess and the Pea

Illustrations by
Ken Bzhelyansky

Adapted by
Books to Bed

Once Upon a Time....

A beautiful Princess was walking in the woods with her pet dragon and mouse. Suddenly, they were surprised by a terrible storm and lost their way.

The dragon and the mouse loved the Princess and wanted to keep her safe. So the dragon, who was big and tall, saw a castle where she might find shelter from the storm.

The dragon was far too big to follow the princess into the castle so he stayed behind in the woods. The little mouse went with the Princess to keep her company and make sure she was safely inside.

When the the Princess, and the little mouse, arrived at the castle the King and Queen who lived there with their very handsome Prince opened the door. Much to their suprise, they found a wet and cold Princess .

The little mouse knew the dragon outside would be worried and he needed a way to let him know what was happening. When he spotted the Royal Owl, he knew the owl could fly to the Dragon. So...
the little mouse
    Told the owl, who
        Told the dragon
            That the princess was safe.

The King and Queen sat with the Princess by the fireplace and heard her sad story of being lost in the storm. Since they were kind people, they immediately invited her to stay overnight.

This Prince had been trying to find a Princess to marry. Although he had searched high and low, he had not been able to find that very special Princess. But now, he thought this wonderful Princess who appeared at his door, might be the perfect one for him to marry. However, the Queen was not so sure...

The little mouse spotted a Royal Dog by the fire, So...

the little mouse

      Told the dog, who

        Told the owl, who

          Told the dragon

            That it was easy to see that the Prince was falling in love.

The Queen believed that the Prince could only marry a Royal
Princess. So she planned a test.

The Queen ordered the most comfortable bed to be made for the royal guest. When twenty featherbeds were laid on top of twenty mattresses, she thought that's enough! She then placed a tiny pea under the mattress at the bottom of the pile. Because she knew a royal secret; a true Princess would feel the pea and not be able to sleep all night.

The little mouse
saw the Royal Cats
    on the bed, So...
        the little mouse,
            Told the cats, who
            Told the dog, who
        Told the owl, who
    Told the dragon
About the Queen's plan and
that the Princess was
    climbing into a
        tall bed with a pea
    under the
            mattress.

The Princess closed her eyes,but as tired as she was, she was not able to fall asleep. She kept tossing and twitching and turning and counting sheep…

14

16

15

17

18

9

11

10

Nothing worked!
As the sun came up she had
barely slept a wink.

8

19

In the morning, the tired Princess dragged herself to breakfast. She looked so exhausted! The Queen knew right away that she was in fact a real Royal Princess!

So the Queen and King gave the Prince their blessing to ask the Princess to marry him.

The little mouse saw the Royal Parrot
in the breakfast room, So...
the little mouse,
Told the parrot, who
Told the cats, who
Told the dog, who
Told the owl, who
Told the Dragon
That Princess passed the True Princess test!

The storm was over and it was a beautiful day. So the Prince and the Princess strolled into the castle garden. There the Prince asked the Princess to marry him.

The little mouse saw
a frog in the garden, So...
the little mouse,
Told the frog, who
Told the parrot, who
Told the cats, who
Told the dog, who
Told the owl, who
Told the Dragon
That the Prince and Princess are in love
and are going to be married.

The Prince and Princess had a wonderful wedding. All the people in the Kingdom came from far and wide to celebrate. But this time, the little mouse did not have to tell the Dragon,

he was right there and knew that the Prince and Princess would live...

...Happily Ever After!

Books to Bed Publications

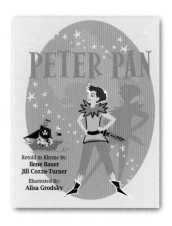

In a faraway place named Neverland
lived a magical boy they called Peter Pan.
Come soar through the sky on a fantastic trip
with mermaids, adventure and Hook's pirate ship!
This timeless story of Pan and his friends
will captivate children from beginning to end!

Retold in Rhyme by Ilene Bauer and Jill Cozza-Turner
Illustrated by Alisa Grodsky

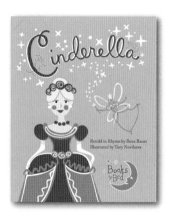

Cinderella was sweet, but sad as could be,
from her selfish stepsisters she wanted to flee.
Join her on a journey of hope and true love
and a tiny glass slipper that fits like a glove.
This classic tale is a helpful reminder
that "good things will come if you treat others kinder."

Retold in Rhyme by Ilene Bauer
Illustrated by Tory Novikova

Casey at the Bat is poem about baseball written in 1888 by Ernest Thayer. In our illustrated version, the excitement of the crowd is personified in our young fan commenting on the game, caught up in the drama of the team's star player striking out. Have fun filling out baseball trivia and brain teasers inside the book!

Adapted by Jill Cozza-Turner
Illustrated by Alisa Grodsky

Books to Bed Publications

"Twas the Night Before Christmas" is a timeless classic that families have shared and loved for nearly 180 years. This heartwarming tale with wonderful images of Santa and his reindeer continues to provide opportunities for families to read together and create holiday traditions both parents and children will remember and enjoy.

Poem by Clement C. Moore
Illustrated by Alisa Grodsky

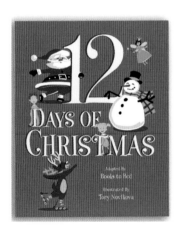

The Twelve Days of Christmas is poem that became a holiday tradition as far back as the sixteenth century. Books to bed updated this wonderful classic with things that twenty-first century kids would love to have for the holidays. Have fun counting and trying to memorize fun Christmas gifts that appear from lots of different family members and friends!

Adapted by Books to Bed
Illustrated by Tory Novikova